The Sweet Treats Carnival

A Scratch-and-Sniff STORY

By Molly Kempf

Illustrated by MJ Illustrations

Grosset & Dunlap

Strawberry Shortcake™ © 2007 by Those Characters From Cleveland, Inc. Used under license by Penguin Young Readers Group. All rights reserved. Published by Grosset & Dunlap, a division of Penguin Young Readers Group, 345 Hudson Street, New York, New York 10014. GROSSET & DUNLAP is a trademark of Penguin Group (USA) Inc. Printed in Thailand.

ISBN 978-0-448-44456-7   10 9 8 7 6 5 4 3 2 1

Visit <u>www.strawberryshortcake.com</u> to join the Friendship Club and redeem your Strawberry Shortcake Berry Points for "berry" fun stuff!

Strawberry Shortcake was berry excited—the day of the Sweet Treats Carnival had arrived at last! She and her friends had been getting ready for weeks. They had each planned special games to play at the carnival—and made sweet treats for the prizes!

"Wow!" exclaimed Strawberry as she arrived at Huckleberry Briar, where the carnival was being held. "It looks just like a real carnival!"

"Ginger and I spent all morning hanging up the balloons and streamers," Huck said proudly. "Can we play my game first? It's called Go Fish." He handed everyone a fishing pole with a sticky piece of tape at the end of the line. Then the kids tried to catch paper fish in a bucket.

"I caught three," said Ginger Snap.

"I caught four!" Strawberry said proudly.

"Rainbow beat us all," Angel Cake laughed. "She's got *eight!*"

"Good job!" said Huck. "Here's your prize—a pack of my favorite wild-berry bubble gum!"

"I caught only one fish," Blueberry Muffin said with a frown.

"That's okay!" Strawberry replied. "There are lots more games to play!"

"You're right," Blueberry said. "Let's play mine next! It's called Hot Muffin. Everybody sits in a circle and passes around this muffin while the music plays. If you're holding the muffin when the music stops, you're out! The last person left wins a prize."

The kids passed the muffin around while Blueberry played the music. When the song stopped, Rainbow Sherbet was caught holding the muffin. Huck was the next one out, followed by Strawberry, Ginger, and Orange. That meant Angel Cake was the winner!

"Yay!" exclaimed Angel as Blueberry handed her the prize— a big bag full of blueberry jelly beans. "I love jelly beans!"

"Strawberry's game looks berry fun," said Ginger. "Can we play that next?"

"Abso-berry-lutely!" Strawberry replied. "Follow me!" She led her pals to a net made of strawberry vines. "Whoever throws the most strawberries through the net wins the prize," Strawberry explained as she handed out baskets of strawberries.

This doesn't look too hard, Blueberry thought. *Maybe I'll win this game!*

But after the kids finished throwing their strawberries, Huck was clearly the winner. He'd made a basket every single time!

"Yes!" Huck cheered. "I love basketball!"

"Don't you mean *strawberry-ball?*" teased Strawberry as she gave Huck a gallon of homemade strawberry ice cream for his prize.

Blueberry tried to laugh with the rest of her friends—but inside, she was disappointed that she hadn't won.

"Let's play my game now," suggested Angel Cake. "It's a cake walk, of course!" She showed her friends a path made of squares that had bright numbers painted on them. "I have the secret number," she explained. "The person standing on the number when the music stops is the winner."

Angel Cake turned on the music, and the kids jumped, hopped, and skipped around the path. Suddenly, the music stopped and everyone froze on a different square.

"The secret number is ten!" Angel announced.

Blueberry looked down. She was standing on 9.

"That's me! I won!" cried Ginger next to her.

"Yay for Ginger!" Angel cheered. "Your prize is a tray of my berry best vanilla cupcakes—with lots of sprinkles, of course!"

Angel's cupcakes are berry yummy, Blueberry thought sadly. *I wish I had won them.*

"Would you like to play my game?" Orange Blossom asked shyly. She showed her friends a glass jar filled with tiny flowers. "Whoever guesses the right number of orange blossoms gets the prize!"

I'm berry good at guessing! thought Blueberry. "Fifty!" she yelled excitedly.

"I guess forty-six," said Strawberry.

"Seventy-five!" Huck called out.

"There are forty-five orange blossoms in the jar," Orange said. "That makes Strawberry the winner!"

I was so close, Blueberry thought sadly. *But I still didn't win.*

"Here's your prize, Strawberry," Orange said as she handed her friend a bunch of orange-flavored lollipops.

"*Mmm!*" Strawberry said. "Thank you—I can't wait to have one!"

The kids played Ginger Snap's game next. She showed them
several pyramids of milk bottles, then handed everyone a beanbag.
"Whoever knocks down the most milk bottles wins," Ginger said.

Blueberry squinted at her pyramid of milk bottles. She aimed her beanbag at the center bottle and threw it as hard as she could—but it flew a little too high and only knocked down the top bottle. As she sighed, Blueberry heard a loud crash. Orange Blossom had knocked down *all* of her milk bottles with one throw!

"Way to go!" Huck said. "You have great aim, Orange!"

"I do?" asked Orange, surprised.

"You sure do!" Ginger replied as she handed Orange her prize— a tray of sweetly spiced ginger cookies.

Rainbow Sherbet's game was the last one. Blueberry held her breath as she watched Rainbow set up a large pole for playing Ring Toss. *I just have to win this one,* she thought.

"Ring Toss is one of my berry favorite games!" Strawberry said as Rainbow passed out rainbow-colored rings. One by one, the kids tried to throw the rings around the pole. Strawberry didn't miss a single one!

"Strawberry is the winner!" Rainbow declared as she gave Strawberry a cone of fluffy cotton candy.

"Thank you, Rainbow!" exclaimed Strawberry. "I love—Blueberry, what's wrong? Why are you crying?"

"I–I–I didn't win a single game!" sobbed Blueberry. "I'm just a big loser!"

Strawberry ran over to Blueberry and gave her a big hug. "Don't be silly!" she cried. "You're not a loser at all! You played fairly, and you were happy for your friends when they won. That makes you a great friend—not a loser." She gave Blueberry some cotton candy and a lollipop. The rest of the kids shared their treats, too.

"Besides, most of those games were based on luck," added Huck. "*Anybody* could have won—or lost."

"That's true," Blueberry said with a smile. "And even if I didn't win today, I'm still pretty lucky—because I have the berry best friends ever!"